For Jake J A, with love ~ M. C. B.

For Kerry James ~ T. M.

Text copyright © M. Christina Butler 2011
Illustrations copyright © Tina Macnaughton 2011
Original edition published in English by Little Tiger Press,
an imprint of Magi Publications, London, England, 2011.

Printed in China • LTP/1800/0335/0911

Library of Congress Cataloging-in-Publication Data is available.

One Christmas Night

M. Christina Butler   Illustrated by Tina Macnaughton

Good Books

Intercourse, PA 17534, 800/762-7171, www.GoodBooks.com

It was nearly Christmas and
Little Hedgehog just could not wait.
"Christmas cookies and cake
– yum yum!" he laughed.
"Oh, now I can put up the big shiny
star that Badger gave me."

"Perfect!" squealed Little Hedgehog as he perched the star on the very top of his tree.

Then he opened Badger's card. "How lovely," he said. It had a huge, glittering Christmas tree on the front.

"Oh dear! My house isn't Christmas-y and my tree doesn't sparkle like that," he sighed.

Just then he heard a *rat-a-tat-tat* at the door.

"Merry Christmas!" cried Mouse.

"Thank you," said Little Hedgehog.

"But Mouse, I don't know what to do!

My house just isn't Christmas-y at all."

"We'll soon fix that," Mouse smiled.

"We can make pinecones sparkle with glitter," said Mouse as they tramped into the woods.

"Take cover!" cried Little Hedgehog as the cones came tumbling down.

"There's holly for the fireplace," Mouse said.
"Ouch!" squeaked Little Hedgehog. "It has
more prickles than me!"

"Chestnuts and acorns and big bowls
of berries!" they all sang as they
marched home.

Together they glued and glittered until nuts
and acorns twinkled like stars, and holly twigs
shimmered red, green, and gold.

"Yippee!" cried Little Hedgehog. "It's like a magic Christmas-y cave!" said Mouse. "But we have to go. We haven't wrapped our presents yet."

"Oh, no!" squeaked Little Hedgehog. "Presents? I've forgotten to get presents for my friends!"

Little Hedgehog thought hard. "I know – I can give this book to Badger."

"I'll make a carrot cake for Rabbit."

"And a night-time picture for Fox."

"I can make stockings full of nuts for my tiniest friends," chuckled Little Hedgehog, pattering into the woods again.

"And a big bunch of twinkly twigs for Mouse," he smiled.

Little Hedgehog wandered on and on through the trees, looking for the best twigs he could find. The woods grew darker and the snowflakes swirled faster around him.

"Phew!" he gasped, struggling
with the basket. "How will I
ever get all of this home?"

At last the snow stopped, and a bright
moon peeped above the trees. Little
Hedgehog huffed and puffed, and then, in
the stillness, he heard a *pad-pad-padding*
noise getting closer and closer, until . . .

...*CRASH!*

"Eek!" yelped Fox, bumping into Little Hedgehog.

"You look like a walking
Christmas tree!"

Little Hedgehog and Fox
chuckled and chattered all
the way back home.

Fox helped to put the presents around the tree.
"Everything looks lovely!" he said.

But Little Hedgehog wasn't sure. "Something is
still missing."

Suddenly there was a loud knock at the door . . .

. . .and in walked Badger with Rabbit and the mice.

"Of course!" squeaked Little Hedgehog, clapping
his paws. "That's what was missing – all of my friends!
Merry Christmas, everyone!"